Famous
Illustrated Tales of
VIKRAM & BETAAL

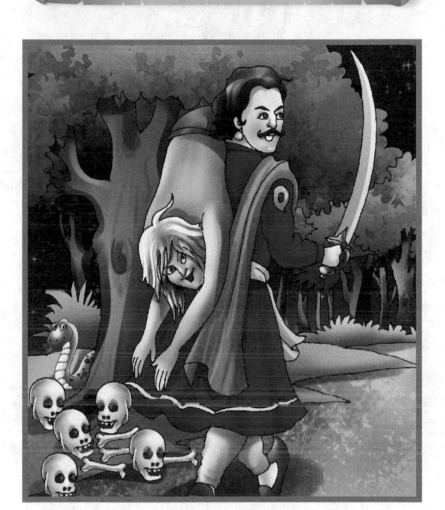

MAPLE KIDS

Famous Illustrated Tales of
VIKRAM & BETAAL

Published by

MAPLE PRESS PRIVATE LIMITED

Corporate & Editorial Office
A 63, Sector 58, Noida 201 301, U.P., India

phone +91 120 455 3581, 455 3583
email info@**maple**press.co.in
website www.**maple**press.co.in

Reprinted 2018

ISBN: 978-93-50339-05-3
Go to www.**maple**library.com for more e-books

Book Layout by Artyfino
Printed in: HT Media Limited, Gr. Noida, India

10 9 8 7 6 5 4 3

Contents

King Vikramaditya Meets Betaal

Many years ago a king called Vikramaditya lived in India. He was known for his wisdom and kindness. But people talked about his bravery.

One day, in the court of the king a strange *tantric* came and presented him with a fruit. The king accepted the fruit. The strange *tantric* asked the king to keep the fruit in his treasury.

The *tantric* again came to the king's court the next day and again presented a fruit. This continued for many years until one day the treasurer came to the court told the king about a mysterious happening.

The king left the court immediately and rushed to his treasury. The fruits that the *tantric* had been presenting to the king over the years had all turned into precious stones. The king and his ministers were overjoyed. They could not believe their eyes.

The next day, when the *tantric* arrived, the king stood from his throne and bowed to him with respect and said,

"O great saint, it is indeed an honor that my court should be graced with your presence. What can I do in return for your blessings?"

The *tantric* said, "My blessings shall always be

with you wise king. But there is something that I must ask you to do."

The great king had never turned away anyone who came to his court seeking his help. He agreed to fulfill the *tantric*'s wish.

The *tantric* said, "Deep in the forest, where most people fear to go, there is a Peepal tree on which hangs the body of a dead man. You must bring me that dead body. I have to offer that corpse to the Goddess for her blessings. You must go to the forest alone, on the next new moon night."

The king started for the Pandabaranya forest at once. As directed by the *tantric*, he began looking for the Peepal tree that stood in the centre of the forest. It was dark inside the forest. But Vikramaditya was brave. He moved on.

The night set in and there was no moon in the sky. The king approached the Peepal tree with sword in his hand. Skulls, skeletons and bones were scattered on the ground under the tree. From a distance, the king saw the dead body. It was thin and white as chalk and hung upside down from a branch.

The king climbed the tree. With great effort, he dragged the corpse through the branches and climbed down from the tree. He then put the corpse around his shoulders and began walking towards home. Suddenly the dead body began laughing. It was ghost.

The king was shocked but he was not scared. He

calmly continued his journey.

The ghost asked, "Who are you?" The king replied, "I'm King Vikramaditya." He asked the ghost "Who are you?" The ghost said, "I am Betaal. Where are you taking me?"

The king told Betaal about the *tantric* and how he had requested the king to bring Betaal to him. Betaal did not seem surprised. He said, "He is a fraud. I was born on the same day and at the same hour as the *tantric*. If the *tantric* gets me, he will use me to increase his powers and then he will kill you to increase his powers further."

The king was in distress. "I have already promised the *tantric* that I would bring you to him. It would not be fair if I failed. I must carry you to him even if my life is at stake," he said. Betaal was impressed with the king. He decided to help him.

He said, "All right then, I will tell you a story at the end of which I will ask you a question. If your answer is wrong, I will come with you. But if you answer it correctly, I will fly back to the tree. However if you choose to be silent, your head will burst into flames. Do you agree?"

Betaal knew that the wise king will always know the answer and he will never lie. Vikramaditya had no choice but to agree. Betaal began to tell a story.

The Four Suitors

Once upon a time a wise king named Udayaditya lived in Mithila. Everyone under his rule respected the king for his sense of justice and equality. They loved him for his kindness.

The king had a daughter. She was known for her beauty and intelligence. Rumors said that princess Rupamanjari was so beautiful that she could make any man fall in love with her.

When she grew up, all the eligible princes in the kingdoms near and far wished to marry her. It was hard for the poor king and his queen to select which of them would be best for their beloved daughter.

Then one day, while the king held the royal court, a very handsome prince approached him and bowed respectfully and said is a deep voice, "I am the prince of Kalinga and I have come to you with a wish in my heart." He said that he desired to marry the princess.

The king said, "I respect your wish young man. Kalinga is our neighbour and ally. I shall be happy to have you as my son-in-law as this shall strengthen the bonds between our kingdoms. But tell me, apart from belonging to a royal family, what do you think makes you special?"

The prince said, "Your majesty, I am a warrior and I have trained with great masters, in various forms of martial arts. I lead the army of my country

as their chief and have won many battles." The king was pleased. He invited the young prince to stay with his family in the palace as a royal guest until the princess made a decision about the proposal.

Next day, as the king was holding his court, another young prince approached him and said that he wished to marry the princess. This young prince introduced himself as the prince of Janakpura and said, "Your majesty, I have read all the religious books. I have spent days searching for the truths of life and of the world. My quest for knowledge makes me special." The king was impressed again. He requested the prince to stay as his royal guest until it was decided.

On the third day, another handsome prince approached the king and said he was from Vaishali. He too said that he wished to marry princess Rupamanjari. He said, "Your majesty, I am gifted by mother nature. I can understand the language of birds and beasts. I understand their joys and their sorrows." The king admired his talent. Like before, he asked this prince too to remain as his guest while the princess made a decision about the proposal.

And there on the fourth day came to the king a prince from Malabya. Like all the three princes who came before him, he too expressed his desire to marry the princess. He claimed, "Your majesty, I come from a rich kingdom where we believe that progress lies in making money. I am a skilled trader. I can make good use of wealth to generate more wealth."

The king and his queen were confused as to which prince amongst the four would make a perfect groom for their daughter. After much thought, they left it to their daughter to decide.

And here, Betaal stopped. He asked, "Great king, now tell me, who do you think should the princess choose? Who should make the right match for her beauty and intelligence?"

Vikramaditya was quick to answer, "If the princess is as intelligent as you tell me, she would select the prince of Kalinga. The prince of Janakpura is a scholar. He cannot be a good king." Betaal nodded. The king continued, "The prince from Vaishali is exceptionally gifted as he can understand the language of the birds and the beasts. But what good is that when his kingdom Is at war? And as for the prince of Malabya, he by virtue is a businessman and no king. If the princess is wise and cares for her people, she would marry the prince of Kalinga as he is a true warrior and during times of war, he will lead his people to peace."

Betaal was laughing again. "You are right, great king. And here I go." With a swift tug, Betaal freed himself from Vikramaditya and flew back to the tree.

The Two Gifted Brothers

Betaal was gleefully swinging from his bough when Vikramaditya reached him and dragged him down from the tree. Putting Betaal around his shoulders he continued his journey.

The thin clouds silently parted in the sky and the stars twinkled from between them. Betaal sighed. He asked, "You don't give up easily. Do you?" The king smiled. Betaal began to tell another story.

Once upon a time a scholarly *brahmin* lived in the city of Pataliputra. He was a gentle and a very pious man. God had blessed him with two sons. Both of them were as gentle and kind as their father. These two sons were extraordinarily talented.

The elder son was gifted with the ability to judge people's character and by so doing could warn the others of their intentions. The younger brother had the ability judge the nature of things by smelling them.

The talents of the two brothers began to be much talked about in the kingdom. The king heard of this and one day they were called to the court.

The king wished to employ them as his special advisors. The brothers agreed.

They began to assist the king in all his decisions. They would often travel with the king on his

diplomatic visits to other kingdoms.

One day, while on one such visit, the king and his party were given a warm welcome by the kingdom. A festival and several programmes were organised in their honor.

The king and his men feasted on the food and wine all night and after that the king wished to take rest. The large royal guest room was richly furnished for him. The king after having a heavy meal wanted nothing but to lay his head on the pillow and close his eyes for a bit.

He entered the room with the brothers behind him. The elder brother said, "Your majesty, I do not trust the king of this kingdom. He is jealous of you and plots to kill you."

The king said, "Nonsense! He has arranged so much to make us comfortable. I don't see how he may be plotting to harm me. I think too much food is making you mad." Then he sat on his bed and leaned to grab the pillow when the elder brother caught his wrist.

"Pardon me your majesty, but I think something is wrong. We must have that pillow checked before you lay your head on it."

The king was confused and irritated. But he could not ignore the elder brother's warning. He asked the younger brother to inspect the pillow. The younger brother who was standing at the door came closer and sniffed the pillow.

The younger brother said, "The pillow is laced with animal hair your highness. Some of those are pretty sharp and shall cut through your skin if you lie on it. The tips are laced with poison that can kill you."

The king did not touch the pillow. He decided to spend the rest of the night without a pillow and next morning he secretly carried the pillow with him and returned to his own kingdom. When he had it checked by experts, they told him that the brothers had been correct. He rewarded the brothers handsomely for their service.

Betaal continued, "Tell me great king, which of the two brothers was wiser and had the greater talent?"

The king smiled. He knew the answer this time too. He said, "The elder one. He was the one who sensed the wrong intentions of their host. He was the one who suspected the pillow first. The younger brother only used his talents to confirm his brother's suspicion."

Betaal was shaking with laughter. He had begun to enjoy the game. He said, "Your judgement is flawless," and he rose and flew back to his tree. An owl hooted and it echoed through the forest.

Ranjabati's Dilemma

Once again, King Vikramaditya climbed the tree and brought Betaal down. Crickets screeched from the bushes and the cool night breeze brushed past them. Lifelessly swinging on the king's shoulder, Betaal began to tell another story.

A rich merchant lived in the capital city of Magadha. He was called Bidhushekhar. Bidhushekhar was known within his community for his wealth and honourable living. He had a son named Rajshekhar.

Rajshekhar had grown up with another young boy called Aviroop. They had always been best friends. People who did not know about them often thought that they were brothers.

As they grew up to be young men, they began to enjoy themselves by travelling in and around the city. One day as they were relaxing on the banks of the river which ran by a temple of Goddess Durga, Rajshekhar spotted a very beautiful girl. He fell in love with her at once.

Aviroop knew who the girl was. He himself had been in love with her for a very long time now. He told his friend that her name was Ranjabati and she belonged to the washerman community.

They began to visit that place every day. Rajshekhar's heart pined for Ranjabati. Aviroop suggested, "Why don't you tell your parents about her?"

Rajshekhar sadly lowered his eyes and said, "They will never understand. They will never agree that I marry a girl from a caste lower to my own. I fear that it will only make them angry." Aviroop felt very sorry for his friend.

Day by day Rajshekhar's love for Ranjabati grew. When he could not take it anymore, he went to the temple and fell at Goddess Durga's feet. "Mother, my love for Ranjabati is killing me. Bless me mother, that I marry Ranjabati. I promise I shall offer you my head on a full moon night."

He began to waste away in love. He stopped eating and his bones began to show. His sickness worried his parents. They wondered what had happened to their son. Aviroop told them that Rajshekhar had fallen in love with Ranjabati and was wasting away because he couldn't marry her without their consent.

Afraid that they might lose their only son Bidhushekhar and his wife agreed to marry Rajshekhar to Ranjabati. The wedding was arranged and the feast continued for the next few days. Rajshekhar recovered from his illness and they lived happily together.

One day when Rajshekhar, Ranjabati and Aviroop were visiting the river where they had first seen Ranjabati, Rajshekhar remembered his promised to Goddess Durga. He decided to wait for a full moon night.

As the next full moon night arrived, he went to the temple. With folded hands and tears in his eyes he thanked the Goddess for her blessings. Then with his sword, he cut his head off.

When Rajshekhar did not come back, Ranjabati began to worry. She sent Aviroop to look for her husband. When Aviroop found his friend in the temple he grieved. He prayed to the Goddess, "Mother, I do not want people to believe that I have murdered my best friend for his beautiful wife. I must also offer myself to you. Please accept my sacrifice." And with Rajshekhar's sword, he cut his head from his body and lay there at the Goddess's feet.

Ranjabati after waiting for a long time grew impatient. She set out herself to find her husband and his friend. When she reached the temple she almost fainted to see the men lying in a pool of blood.

She prayed, "Mother, since my husband is no more in this world I do not have any purpose left." As she was about to plunge the sword into her chest, there was a mysterious light and the Goddess appeared.

"Dear girl, I am very pleased with the sacrifices of these humble men. Do not kill yourself. I shall return their lives to you. As soon as you place their heads on their bodies, they will come back to life."

Goddess Durga disappeared. Overwhelmed with joy, Ranjabati placed the heads on the bodies and the men came back to life. But in her excitement, Ranjabati had exchanged the heads, placing Aviroop's head on Rajshekhar's body and Rajshekhar's head on Aviroop's body.

Betaal said, "Great king, who do you think should Ranjabati take for her husband?"

The king was lost in thoughts. "Ranjabati should choose the body with Rajshekhar's head. Head is most important as it holds a man's personality, character and identity."

Betaal knew the king would answer it wisely. "You are right again," he said and he laughed as he flew towards the tree.

An Example of Generosity

King Vikramaditya was getting tired of Betaal's game but he was determined to take Betaal with him even if he had to spend the night climbing up and down the tree. He put Betaal around his shoulders again and set on his journey.

Betaal was enjoying himself very much. "How long do you wish to keep this up?" he asked. "It depends on you," the king answered. Betaal shook with laughter. "All right, I will begin the story then."

Long ago, there lived a rich merchant named Chandrapati in a city called Mahabalipur. He had a beautiful daughter named Madhumala. One day Madhumala was attending a social event when a handsome young man named Aditya saw her and fell in love with her. Madhumala too was charmed by the young man's sweet nature and wit.

Their love grew with time until one day Aditya decided to marry Madhumala. He went to her father seeking his permission and blessings. But Chandrapati had already promised to wed his daughter to a wealthy young merchant named Sarbajyoti. Aditya was heart-broken.

After days of living with the sorrow, he finally decided to forget Madhumala. However, Madhumala

who had loved Aditya could not do so. She silently protested against her father's wishes. But Madhumala had to marry Sarbajyoti for had she not she would have earned her family a bad name.

The day before the marriage took place, she wrote to Aditya promising him that she will come to him after the marriage and shall live with him thereafter. On the night she was alone with her husband for the first time, Madhumala opened her heart to Sarbajyoti and told him everything. Sarbajyoti realized that there was no use trying to persuade her as she already loved someone else. He allowed her to leave.

Madhumala left her home still dressed in her bridal *saree* and ornaments. On her way a thief crossed her path. "Give me all your jewels or I will hurt you," he threatened. "Please let me go good sir," Madhumala begged. "I am in a hurry to go to my lover. I promise I will give you all my jewels when I have met him." The thief did not believe her but he let her go.

Madhumala reached Aditya's home and knocked on the door. Aditya appeared at the door and was pretty shocked to see Madhumala. He was angry that she had left her husband to come to him. "What were you thinking? You are a married woman now. I cannot have someone else's wife to live with me. You must go back to your husband. There is no place for you here." And he closed the door on her.

Madhumala begged and cried in vain. At last with a heavy heart she decided to go back. On her way she met the thief again. She began to unhook her jewels to give to him.

The thief had noticed her tears. He asked, "What bothers you lady?" Madhumala told him the whole story. The thief was sorry for her. He did not take her jewels and saw that she safely reached her home.

When Madhumala reached home Sarbajyoti was upset upon seeing her. He said, "I am sorry, I cannot have you back as my wife. You left my home to live to another man. I do not trust you anymore and thus cannot have you back. You must leave."

All hell broke loose for Madhumala. She now had nowhere to go. Fearing the shame that this would bring her she went to the river nearby and ended her life.

Betaal stopped. He asked, "Who do you think made the greatest sacrifice?"

The king replied, "It is only when you give up something willingly and selflessly it is called a sacrifice. Aditya gave up Madhumala's love but he did it for a reason. Madhumala was somebody's wife and he could not have somebody's wife living with him. Sarbajyoti let go of Madhumala but he would not have her back because he did not trust her. Madhumala on the other hand gave up her life but it was because she was afraid of the shame her condition would bring her. We cannot call these as sacrifices. Only the thief made the sacrifice. Robbing people was how he earned his livelihood. But he let go of Madhumala's jewels because he took pity in her. His act of humanity truly sets an example of what sacrifice is."

"I was expecting that you would give me the right answer," Betaal said. Vikramaditya turned around and began walking towards the tree as the ghost flew back to its branches.

The Delicate Queens

During the time of King Debmalya who ruled Puruspur, the people of the city praised their king for his bravery and wisdom. But his three queens were the ones they talked about the most. The gentle king loved all three of his wives very much. But there was something strange about those women.

One day when King Debmalya was strolling in the garden with his first wife Subhalaxmi, a soft pink flower fell from a tree and brushed past the queen's hand. The queen shrieked and fainted. The worried king ordered for all the good doctors of the city to attend on her. They found, the queen's skin was so delicate that the soft pink flower had managed to badly hurt her hand. They advised that she stayed in bed for few days.

Another tragedy happened that night when the king was relaxing in one of the balconies of his palace with his second wife Chandrawati. Cool breeze carried the fragrance from the flowers in the garden to them as the moon bathed the balcony with its beams. It was the perfect romantic night when the queen began to scream. She shouted, "I can't bear the moon beams on my skin, It is burning me!"

The puzzled king had to draw the curtains to keep the moon out. The physicians were called

again. They advised that she applied sandalwood paste all over and rested.

Mrinalini, the king's third wife was the most beautiful of the three. One day the king wished to see her. As she was walking from her room to the king's she suddenly burst into cries and fainted. The physicians were called and they found that her hands were covered in blisters. When she gained her senses, she told them that, it was the sound of rice being pounded that came from the kitchens. It was unbearable.

"Now tell me king, who amongst the three queens was the most sensitive?" Betaal asked.

The king spoke slowly, "It has to be the third queen. All of the three queens were no doubt delicate but for Subhalaxmi and Chandrawati, the flower and the moon had directly touched their skin. For Mrinalini however, she was hurt by just the sound of rice being pounded. She is the most delicate of them all."

Betaal said, "You are right," and he flew back to the tree.

King Mahendra's Justice

King Vikramaditya climbed the tree again and brought Betaal down. Betaal was silently admiring his patience. After they had walked few paces from the tree he began to tell a story. It was about a king who was as patient and generous as Vikramaditya.

Once upon a time in the kingdom of Varanasi, ruled a king called Mahendra. He was a noble king. A man of principle he had high regards for moral values. His subjects regarded him as an able ruler and loved him for his generosity.

In that same city, there lived a rich merchant called Dhanamalya. He was famous far and wide for his trading skills and enormous wealth.

Dhanamalya had a young daughter. People said she was so beautiful that even the maidens in heaven were jealous of her. That her long hair was as black as the moonless night and her skin was as smooth and white as milk. They also said that her nature was as gentle as a deer in the forest.

In no time the king heard these rumors. He decided to marry this girl his people were talking about. But first he had to be sure that the girl was indeed beautiful and worthy. He sent for two of his trusted servants and ordered them "Visit the merchant's home and meet his daughter. Find out

if she is really as beautiful as people say. Judge her character and let me know if she is fit to be a queen." The servants bowed to their king and left.

Commanded by their king the servants reached the merchant's house in disguise. They made an excuse to see his daughter. When she appeared before them, they were amazed by her beauty and charm. It was exactly as the rumors had described. The first servant exclaimed "Oh! What a beauty! The king must marry her." The second servant agreed, "You are right. I have never met a girl more beautiful than her. I am sure the king will not be able to take his eyes off her."

Then they thought for a while. The second servant said, "Do you think, if the king married her he might get distracted from his duties?" The first servant agreed. "Perhaps there are. This girl's beauty may bewitch our king and he might then neglect his people and his kingdom." So they decided to never tell the king how extraordinarily beautiful the girl was.

The king trusted his servants. He believed them when they told him that the rumors were not true and that the girl's beauty was ordinary. He was heart-broken. One day Dhanamalya himself approached the king with the proposal of marrying his daughter to him. But the king was so upset that he refused the proposal without a second thought.

Dhanamalya was disappointed. He then arranged to get his daughter married to one of the king's courtiers. Days passed. The marriage took place and life moved on.

One day, the king was passing by this courtier's house in his royal chariot. Suddenly, he spotted a woman standing at the window. The woman was so beautiful that the king liked her at once. He asked his charioteer, "Who is this lady standing at that window? I have never seen any woman more beautiful than her."

"Your majesty," the charioteer replied, "She is the only daughter of the rich merchant Dhanamalya. People say she is so beautiful that even the maidens of the heaven are jealous of her. She is now married to one of the courtiers in your court."

The king was angry. "If what you tell me is true, then it can only mean that the two servants had lied to me. Bring them to me at once! I will have them put to death."

When the two servants were brought to the king they fell at his feet and begged for his mercy. They revealed their intentions to him but the king did not pay any attention to them. He ordered that both of them must be put to death immediately.

"Dear king," Betaal said as he had finished his story. "Tell me, do you believe King Mahendra's decision to put those two men to death was justified?"

Vikramaditya replied, "A servant's duty is to obey his master. It was right that the servants be punished. It was their duty to report to the king of what they had seen. They had failed to do it. However, their intentions were for the well-being of the king and the kingdom. Their act was selfless. In light of this, it was not justified that the king had them put to death."

Betaal whispered, "Brave king, you are right again." He glided with the wind, towards the Peepal tree.

The Courtier

Vikramaditya dragged Betaal down from the tree again. As they set off for their journey, Betaal began his story.

Long ago, King Punyabrata ruled the vast kingdom of Manikyapur. The king was loved by his people for he was kind-hearted and wise.

Punyabrata was a brave king. He had won many kingdoms with his clever strategies and bravery in the battlefield. He was also a passionate hunter. The king often enjoyed riding into the forests near his kingdom in search of rabbits, pigeons and deer.

One day, he lost his way while chasing a beautiful spotted deer in the forest. The deer had managed to escape and the king was left behind to find his way back home.

The king strolled in the forest for hours but could not find the way. It was beginning to get dark. He grew hungry, thirsty and tired. Frustrated, he got down from his horse and sat under a tree when suddenly he saw someone coming towards him with a small lamp in his hand.

The alert king grabbed the hilt of

his sword. He was ready to put up a fight. But then the king realized it was a young man who had come to help him.

The young man said, "I believe your majesty has lost his way." The king replied, "You are right." The young man spoke again, "I have brought some food and water. Please eat and rest. We shall find the way out of this forest tomorrow." And the young man made his humble offering to the king. The king ate and then lay down under the tree. Sleep came over him.

When the king got up next morning, he noticed that the young man had been awake all night. He had been guarding the king with a stick in his hand. The king was impressed with the young man's service. The king asked, "What is your name?" The young man replied, "Pratap, your majesty." Then the king offered, "Would you like to be in my service as one of my courtiers?" Pratap agreed and was overjoyed.

They finally crossed the forest and reached the royal palace. From then on, Pratap remained in the palace as one of the courtiers.

Days passed. Pratap was happy and content. Once morning, he decided to visit the forest where he had met the king for the first time. Suddenly he spotted a very beautiful girl. He fell in love instantly. He wished to marry her.

The girl was not sure about the proposal. She said, "Come back tomorrow and I will let you know

what I have decided." Pratap dreamt about her all night. In the morning he went to the king and told him everything.

The kind king agreed to go with Pratap to the forest. They reached the forest and found the girl was waiting for them. But when she saw the king her expressions changed. She bowed to the king and said, "I had not hoped to see your majesty here. Please, marry me and make me your queen."

Both the king and Pratap were shocked. Pratap said, "Your majesty, even though I wish to marry this woman, she is fit to be your queen. If your majesty wishes to take this woman for his wife, I shall happily sacrifice my love."

The king was pleased by his courtier's devotion. He turned to the girl and said, "Fair lady, this young man has fallen in love with you. I cannot marry a woman who has been chosen by one of my courtiers. Pratap has always been faithful to me. He shall take good care of you. As his wife, you can enjoy luxuries as both of you would be living in the royal palace."

The wedding was arranged and Pratap and the girl were married amidst a big feast. From then on, they lived happily ever after.

It was time for Betaal to ask his question. "Tell me, who was more noble? Was it the king or his courtier?" he asked.

King Vikramaditya answered, "Both the king and his courtier were equally noble. While Pratap was willing to sacrifice his love for the king's sake, the king refused the proposal because his courtier had chosen the girl for himself. But I should say, the king's act qualifies as greater because being the supreme ruler, he could have easily married the girl. This shows the high regards he had for moral values. It suits a king."

Betaal freed himself and began gliding with the wind, towards the tree.

The Bitter Truth

Again king Vikramaditya climbed the tree and brought Betaal down.

Betaal started laughing at the king's condition. Vikramaditya remained silent. "All right king, here is another story for you," he said when he had laughed enough to realize that the king was not paying any attention to the mockery. He continued his story.

Once upon a time, King Chandradhar ruled over the country of Vaishali. He was a generous king. It was said that, whoever came to his court seeking his help, was never turned away.

One day, a poor *brahmin* approached the king with his two young sons. His sons were blind. After respectfully bowing to the king the *brahmin* said, "You majesty, I am so poor that I cannot afford to even feed my sons. They will die if we continue like this for a long time. Please, give me ten pieces of gold so that I may start a business of my own."

The king felt sorry for the thin boys and their poor father. He immediately ordered his treasurer to give the *brahmin* the ten gold pieces. The king asked, "When do you plan to return the

money?" "Within a year your majesty, I shall surely be able to return this loan," the *brahmin* replied. But the king was not satisfied. "And what if you disappeared with the money?" he asked again. "Your majesty may keep my sons in his court until I return with the money," the *brahmin* offered.

The king began to wonder. How could the two blind brothers be of use to him? The *brahmin* assured the king, "My sons have special abilities. The elder one can tell you the breed and nature of any horse that he touches and smells. The younger one can identify and tell you about any gem that he holds in his hand." The king was pleased and it was decided that the brothers would live in the palace with the king until their father paid back the loan.

One day a trader approached the king with a fine horse. The horse seemed quite healthy and strong. The king was impressed. He had almost decided to buy it from the trader when he remembered about the blind *brahmin* boy who lived in his palace. He sent for the elder brother.

The elder brother when he touched and sniffed the horse told the king that the horse was a nervous one and would throw off anyone who tried to ride it. The king had to test it. He ordered one of his courtiers to ride the horse. When the man mounted it the horse kicked and snapped and threw the poor man off its back. The king was pleased with the elder brother and rewarded him handsomely.

One day, the king wished to buy some jewels. He called upon the jeweller and asked him to show some gems. Out of all the gems the jeweller had, the king selected a large diamond. But before he paid the jeweller, he sent for the younger of the blind brothers.

The boy when he held the diamond immediately told the king of its reality. "Your majesty, the diamond is cursed. Whoever wears it would die soon." The puzzled king looked at the jeweller for an explanation. The jeweller confessed, "He is right your majesty. All the three previous owners of this diamond had died suddenly and in very mysterious ways." The king bought a large ruby instead and rewarded the younger brother handsomely.

As the year ended, the *brahmin* approached the king with one thousand gold pieces. He had been successful in his business. The king asked the *brahmin* if he too like his sons had any special ability. The *brahmin* replied that he had. He could see a person's past by holding his hand. The king demanded that the *brahmin* said something about his past.

After holding the king's hand for a moment the *brahmin* said, "You majesty, though you are the worthy ruler of this large kingdom, your father had been a thief who had looted many cities."

The king was furious. "Liar! How dare you say such a thing about me, standing in my court?" He ordered the guards to take the *brahmin* and his sons away and though the *brahmin* had told the truth, both he and his sons were put to death.

"Tell me king, who do you think was responsible for their deaths?" the Betaal asked.

Vikramaditya answered, "The *brahmin* himself was responsible for his own and his sons' deaths. He should have been wiser while telling the king the bitter truth. The king knew he was the son of a thief. But to have it told to him in public was embarrassing and harmful for his authority. It was understood that the *brahmin* would have to face a death sentence."

Betaal's laughter echoed through the forest. "I am impressed by your judgement," he said as he returned to the tree.

Ugrasil and King Brisabhanu

Long ago, there ruled in the kingdom of Madhupura a kind-hearted king called Brisabhanu. He was a wise ruler and people in his kingdom lived in peace and harmony.

However, just outside his kingdom was a vast and dense forest. There in this forest lived a gang of robbers led by a fierce man called Ugrasil. The gang often terrorized the villages near their forest and killed people after looting them. The people of Madhupura were very disappointed for they had to constantly live in fear.

The robbers were so clever that they always covered their faces with the ends of their turbans so that no one would be able to recognize them. No matter how much the king's soldiers tried, they could never catch these robbers as no one could describe the robbers to them.

Years passed and nothing could be done to catch the wicked robbers. Meanwhile, Ugrasil had fallen in love and married a very beautiful girl. His wife was a kind woman and she never supported Ugrasil's wicked ways. She wished that her husband would leave behind his profession. She often tried to tell him this. But it was in vain, for Ugrasil never listened to her.

When they had a beautiful son, a change in Ugrasil's character began to show. He became gentle and would often spare the women and children when they robbed a village. He loved his son very much.

One day when Ugrasil was resting after a meal, he dreamt that the king's guards had caught him and that they had thrown his wife and his son into the river. He woke up sweating. He decided that he would give up this life of a thief and make an honest living. He called a meeting with his gang members and told them this.

"But captain, you cannot do this!" they exclaimed. "We would be lost without you." His gang did not wish that he left them. It could be dangerous for them if he surrendered. And soon Ugrasil found out that they were plotting to kill him.

Fearing for his life and his family's safety, he ran from the forest that night and reached the royal palace in the city. There he asked his wife to wait with his son as he climbed the walls and entered the king's bedroom through the window.

He touched the king's feet and begged for mercy. The king woke at once. "Guards! Thief! Guards!" He began to shout. The guards were quick to act. They came in and immediately captured Ugrasil. Ugrasil said with folded hands, "Great king, I am no thief. I have a wife and a son and I have nowhere to go. I have come here to confess my deeds and beg for your mercy." On hearing the man and seeing the tears in his eyes, the king calmed down. He asked the guards to let go of Ugrasil. Ugrasil confessed everything and promised to tell the whereabouts of the other members of his gang. The king understood. He produced a little bag of money and gave it to Ugrasil. "Go with this money and make an honest living. You are free to leave the city if you promise to return within a year and show me that you have quit your evil ways."

Ugrasil's joys knew no bounds. He took the money, touched the king's feet once more and left the city with his family that very night. Betaal asked Vikramaditya, "Great king, do you think the king made the right decision to pardon the cruel thief?"

Vikramaditya said, "King Brisabhanu's act is a noble example of wisdom and kindness. The purpose of punishment is to make the culprit realize their mistake. Since Ugrasil had already realized his mistake, it was right that the king should pardon him. This might set an example for the other robbers when they hear of it. And they too might want to surrender."

Vikramaditya's answer made Betaal rise from his shoulders once more and fly towards the tree. The king turned around and began chasing him.

Merchant's Daughter and Thief

The next story Betaal told Vikramaditya, was about a beautiful daughter of a merchant.

Once upon a time there lived a rich merchant. He had a daughter. Her name was Chanchala. Though Chanchala was beautiful and intelligent, she was also very fickle minded. Her father tried his best to change her habit but he failed. Disappointed he decided to get her married and sent her away.

A handsome groom was chosen for her and she left her home to live with her husband. Her husband, who was a merchant, often had to go on business trips. So he was away from his home most of the time. One day, her father sent a messenger, to find out how his daughter was doing in her new home.

When the messenger arrived, Chanchala's husband was not at home. Chanchala welcomed the messenger and served him food and wine. She had fallen in love with the man. The messenger too, seemed to like her very much. They began to have an affair.

As days passed, the messenger grew jealous of her husband. He wanted to live with her. Chanchala feared that all hell would break loose if her husband

found out about the affair. She thought of a plan.

Chanchala bought some poison and mixed it with some fruit juice. She then gave the fruit juice to her lover. Not suspecting her, he drank the juice and soon died of the poison. Clever Chanchala dragged the body to a dark corner and hid it there.

When her husband returned, he did not notice the body in the house. When they were having dinner, she began to scream, "Help help! Murder murder!"

The neighbours dashed into their house and found the dead messenger. They informed the guards who captured the husband and produced him before the king.

Murder in that kingdom was punishable by death. When they were dragging him to the gallows, a thief approached the king and bowed. "I am a humble thief your majesty. On the night of the murder, I was hiding inside the house waiting for an opportunity to steal things. I saw that not this man, but his wife mixed poison in fruit juice and gave it to the messenger who died because of it. I beg you to please release this man as he is innocent."

The king released the husband and put Chanchala to death instead.

Betaal paused. "Tell me, who do you think was responsible for the misfortune?"

Vikramaditya answered, "Chanchala's father, the merchant was the only one responsible for the misfortune. Had he told Chanchala's husband of his daughter's bad habit, he would have been more cautious and would have never left his wife alone."

Betaal was smiling. The king had been right. He said, "Here I go again!" And he flew back to the Peepal tree.

The Sage Who Wept and Laughed

Once upon a time a very pious *brahmin* lived in the city of Udaypur. He and his wife made an honest living. They had enough to live by comfortably. But they often wished they had a child. So they spent their days praying to Almighty.

One day, his wife gave birth to a baby boy. Their happiness knew no bounds. They held a feast for the poor and thanked the Almighty for his blessings.

The old *brahmin* and his wife worked to provide their son with the best education. They also taught him the lessons of love, and kindness. Therefore, the boy grew up to be a fine young man.

Everyone in the city talked about the boy's knowledge and wisdom. When he was of age, the *brahmin* and his wife began to look for a bride to get him married. But one day their son fell sick. The *brahmin* and his wife consulted the best doctors and prayed to the Almighty. But it was all in vain. After lying on his bed for a month, the boy died. His dead body was carried to his funeral. The *brahmin* and his wife grieved.

Hearing their loud cries, a sage who was meditating under a tree nearby approached them.

He saw the dead young man lying on the ground while his parents were crying over him. The sage had an idea. "I can easily leave my old body and enter this young man's body," he thought. The sage went back to where he sat, wept for some time, then laughed for some time and finally closed his eyes in concentration.

Just then the young man opened his eyes. The *brahmin* and his wife were surprised. They held their son to their chest and wept in happiness.

Betaal asked the king, "Can you tell me why the sage had first wept and then laughed?"

King Vikramaditya said, "The sage first wept because he was leaving his old body. He then laughed because he was going to enter a strong young body leaving his weak old body behind."

Betaal told the king that he was right again and flew back to the tree.

Story of Two Fathers

King Vikramaditya had to keep his promise to the *tantric*. He climbed the tree again and brought Betaal down. Betaal began to tell him another story.

Long ago a *brahmin* lived in Avantipur. The *brahmin's* wife had died at childbirth and she had left him a beautiful daughter. The *brahmin* loved his daughter very much. He worked day and night and tried his best to make his daughter happy. Bishakha, the *brahmin's* daughter grew up to be a very beautiful and intelligent woman. She also loved her father very much.

One day, when Bishakha was sleeping, a man quietly climbed into her room through the open window and hid behind the curtains. Bishakha was scared. She asked, "Who are you?" The man replied, "I am a thief. The king's guards are after me. Please help me. I promise I will not harm you."

When the king's guards knocked on her door, Bishakha told them that she did not know anything. They were forced to leave. The thief who was hiding in her room was saved. He thanked her and quietly left, through the way he had come.

They often saw each other at the market. They had begun to fall in love. So one day they decided to get married. Bishakha was scared that her father would be very angry because she wanted to marry

a thief. So she decided not to tell him and secretly married the man.

They were happy for some time until one day the thief was caught by the king's guards and sentenced to death for robbing a rich man's house. Bishakha was shattered for she was carrying his child in her womb. When the thief died Bishaka's father got her married to another man and in few months the baby boy was born.

This man accepted the boy as his own. Bishakha died when the boy was only five years old. The man took up the role of a responsible father and the boy grew up to be kind and intelligent. They had loved each other a lot but then one day the man died too.

As he grieved for his father, the boy decided to pray for both his parents' souls. He went to the river and walked into the water. As he was about to offer his prayers, three hands came out of the water.

One hand was wearing bangles. It said, "Son, I am your mother." The young man offered his prayers to his mother. But he was confused about the other two hands. One of them said, "Son, I am your father who has given birth to you." The third hand was silent. When the young man asked, it said, "Son, I am your father too, the one who has brought you up with love and care."

Betaal asked, "Great king, tell me now, who out of the two fathers should the son offer his prayers to?"

Vikramaditya said, "The father who had brought him up. He had fulfilled the duties of a father. If he had not cared for the child when his mother died the child would have died too. Only he has the right to be called as the young man's father."

Betaal sighed. The king was right again. Betaal flew away from Vikramaditya's shoulders and went back to the tree.

When Dreams Come True

Vikramaditya climbed the tree once again and brought Betaal down from it. Betaal was ready with his story. He began to tell it, once they had started walking through the forest.

Once upon a time a rich merchant called Satyapaul lived in Patliputra. Satyapaul had a distant relative who had been orphaned at a very young age. This young boy was called Chandranath.

Though Chandranath lived in Satyapaul's house, he was treated as a servant. This often made him sad. Day after day he dreamt of becoming a rich man.

One afternoon, while he was taking a little nap, he dreamt that he had become a very rich merchant and that Satyapaul now worked as his servant. He began to talk in his sleep. "Hey Satyapaul, you dirty fool. Come here and take my shoes off!"

Just then Satyapaul was crossing by his room. He heard Chandranath's mumblings and was furious. Angry, Satyapaul threw a shoe at Chandranath and chased him away from his home.

Poor Chandranath had nowhere to go. He roamed in the streets all day. He was upset at the humiliation and began to plot revenge. Finally hungry and tired he reached the forest.

A hermit lived in the forest. Chandranath

approached him and touched his feet. The hermit asked, "Why are you so miserable, son?" Chandranath told him everything. The hermit took pity in him. He said, "I will teach you a mantra. If you chant this mantra after you have seen a dream, your dream will come true." And the hermit taught Chandranath the mantra.

As Chandranath was about to leave, the hermit warned, "However, you would be able to use the mantra only three times." Chandranath was puzzled but he was far too happy to complain. Upon returning to the city, he found a small hut and lay down at its steps. Sleep came over him soon and he began to dream.

Chandranath dreamt that Satyapaul was apologizing to him and that he offered to marry Chandranath to his daughter Satyabati. Chandranath woke up. He thought, "I really like what I saw in my dream. Perhaps it is time that I checked whether the mantra works." He began to chant the mantra.

Satyapaul had been looking for Chandranath. He saw Chandranth sitting on the footsteps of the hut. Satyapaul apologized to Chandranath for chasing him away and treating him like a servant. He then offered his daughter as a bride to Chandranath. Chandranath could not believe his ears. The mantra had worked. His dream had come true.

Chandranath accepted the proposal and married Satyabati. Satyapaul offered to set up a business for Chandranath so that they may live comfortably and be happy.

One day Chandranath dreamt that his business had flourished and that he was now the richest merchant in the city. When he woke up, he decided to chant the mantra. Soon his business flourished and he made a lot of money. He became the richest merchant in the city exactly as he had dreamt.

The other merchants in the city were jealous of him. They began to talk about Chandranath's business and how he evaded his taxes in order to be rich. These talks soon became rumours and reached the king's ears. The king got his guards to investigate and found the rumours were true. As a punishment, Chandranath was ordered to pay ten times the amount of the tax he had evaded.

It angered Chandranath. That night he dreamt that he had become the King of Patliputra and that he was punishing all the merchants who had spread the rumors about him. He woke up in the morning and just as he was about to chant the mantra for the last time he realized something.

Chandranath wept. He did not chant the mantra. He went straight to the hermit in the forest and asked him to take away the powers. The hermit smiled as he heard this.

Betaal asked, "Why did Chandranath not chant the mantra and become the King of Patliputra?"

Vikramaditya answered, "Chandranth had realized that without hard work, fame and success mean nothing. It is no fun in living a life where all your dreams easily come true. Through the powers of the mantras, the hermit had taught him this valuable lesson."

Betaal laughed. "You are incredible, great king. I am so sorry I will have to leave again." And he flew back to the tree.

The Most Deserving

When King Vikramaditya went to fetch Betaal again, the ghost was amused. "Dear king, you must be bored of dragging me down again and again," he said. The king remained silent. The ghost continued, "All right, I shall tell you another story. It will keep the boredom away." And Betaal began to tell another story.

Once upon a time, a very pious *brahmin* lived in the kingdom of Kanuj. He had a young daughter named Vidruma. People said that her face was like the moon and her color was like molten gold. Vidruma was very beautiful.

In that same city, there were three very learned young *brahmins*. All three of them loved her very much. They had even approached her father on several occasions to seek her as their wife. But the Brahmin had refused all of them.

One day Vidruma fell very sick. The old *brahmin* tried everything to save her but alas! She died due to her illness. The three young *brahmins* were very disappointed by her death. They wept for days and finally decided to dedicate their lives to her memory.

The first young *brahmin* built a hut near the cemetery and made a bed out of her ashes. He then began to spend his days begging for food and sleeping on the bed.

The second *brahmin* collected Vidruma's bones and dipped them in the holy waters of the Ganges. He then began spending his life living by the side of the river, under the stars.

The third young *brahmin* decided to live the life of a monk. He wandered from village to village, begging for food and shelter. One day when he was visiting a village, a simple trader invited him to spend the night in his house.

When they sat down for dinner, the trader's little boy began to cry very loudly. No matter how much his mother tried to calm him, he kept on crying. Finally the woman was irritated. She picked up her son and threw him into the stove. The boy quickly burnt to ashes.

The young *brahmin* was horrified by the whole event. Trembling with anger he got up from where he sat before his plate of food and said, "You people are so cruel to kill an innocent child. I will not eat in this house for it shall be a sin."

His host begged him to stay. "Please forgive us O great monk. I pray you to stay so that you may see no cruelty has taken place. I can bring my son back to life. He is perfectly safe." The man then fetched a tiny book of prayers and chanted some mantras. The beautiful boy rose from the ashes, alive and hearty.

The *brahmin* was amazed. He could not believe his eyes. Suddenly he had an idea. When his host went to bed, the Brahmin quietly took the book of prayers and left the village to come home.

He was planning to bring Vidruma back to life. But for that he would need her ashes and her bones. He went to the cemetery where the other two *brahmins* were living. "Brothers," he said, "I have found a way of bringing the beautiful Vidruma back to life. But I would need her bones and her ashes." The two *brahmins* were overjoyed to hear this. They brought her ashes and her bones and placed it before the third *brahmin*. The third *brahmin* then began to chant the mantra and soon Vidruma rose from her ashes. She looked more beautiful than she used to. The three *brahmins* were very happy.

But they began to fight amongst themselves as to who should marry her. Betaal stopped and asked the king, "Tell me king, who do you think deserved the most to be her husband?"

King Vikramaditya said, "The first *brahmin*." Betaal was smiling. "The third *brahmin* brought the mantra to bring her back to life. He did the duty that a father should do. The second *brahmin* kept her bones. He did what a son would do. But the first *brahmin* slept with her ashes. It is what a lover would do. Thus he deserved the most to marry her."

Betaal said, "You are right." And he flew back to the Peepal tree.

King Bhoja Finds Vikramaditya's Throne

After many such attempts, it was Betaal who was forced to give up and go to the *tantric* with Vikramaditya. The story of King Vikramaditya and Betaal, went down in history as one of the greatest examples of patience, determination and wisdom.

Many years later, a king called Bhoja, who ruled over the great city of Ujjaini was told about this great king. However, what was interesting was how he found out about king Vikramaditya.

Many years after king Vikramaditya's rule, the great king Bhoja, who ruled the city of Ujjaini went hunting in the forests around his city with some of his men. The wild animals from the forests were disturbing the peace of some villages nearby. So the king decided to kill the animals and restore the peace.

They had spent all day in the forest chasing the animals. When it was mid day and the sun began to shine mightily above them, they decided to rest for a while. They began looking for a spot to rest.

After searching for a long time, they came across a large field. The corn that grew in that field looked delicious. The king was impressed. He began to look for the owner.

They spotted him sitting at the center of the

field, on a mound of earth. When they approached him, he stood up and bowed. "I am honored that you have graced my fields with your presence, your majesty. I am Saravana Bhatta and I own these fields. Please feel free to rest and feast on the corn."

The king and his men were delighted. They set up camp in the field and began to feast on the sweet, juicy corn.

When Saravana Bhatta got down from the mound and saw that the king and his men were feasting on his crops he grew furious. He went to the king and said, "Your majesty, I am a poor man. This corn is my livelihood. If you and your men eat my crop how will I feed my family?" The king offered Saravana Bhatta some money in return for his favor. The farmer thanked the king and went back to his mound.

Strangely when the farmer sat on the mound again, he said, "Your majesty, you rule over these lands. These are more your fields than mine and these are your crops. I am disappointed that you should pay me for what belongs to you. I refuse to take this money." And he returned the money to the king.

The king was now confused. He realized, there was something wrong with the mound. He offered to buy the field from Saravana Bhatta. After having paid a huge price, he ordered the mound to be dug. To everyone's astonishment, the men discovered a large golden throne buried in the mound.

It was a beautiful peacock throne. It was made of solid gold and was studded with precious stones and thirty two strange looking dolls. The king fell in love with the throne at once. He wished it to be carried back to the palace.

But they could not move the throne. The king ordered for more men. But the throne seemed to be magical. It got heavier and heavier making it impossible to be moved. Then one wise advisor suggested, "Your majesty, this throne seemed to have belonged to a great king. We must worship the throne before trying to move it." The king agreed and a team of *brahmins* were called who performed a ritual around the throne. It helped and the throne finally moved.

They brought the throne to the palace and on an auspicious day, the king having finished his morning duties decided to sit on the throne. However no sooner had he stepped on the pedestal, one of the dolls started laughing very loudly. "Wait O king, do you think you have got what it takes to sit on this throne?"

The king was taken by surprise. He said, "Pardon me, I do not understand." "This throne had belonged to the great king Vikramaditya. It takes only greatness like his to sit on this throne. Do you think your wisdom and justice matches that of great king Vikramaditya?"

"Tell me. How great was king Vikramaditya? I want to know more about him" Bhoja demanded.

The doll laughed, "I will tell you a story and you shall judge for yourself, how great king Vikramaditya was." And the doll began to tell a story about king Vikramaditya's greatness. King Bhoja sat wide eyed as he heard the story. He realized, his wisdom and justice were no match for Vikramaditya. King Vikramaditya was indeed a great king.